Mountain Man's Obsession

Cameron Hart

Published by Cameron Hart, 2024.

This is a work of fiction. Similarities to real people, places, or events are entirely coincidental.

MOUNTAIN MAN'S OBSESSION

First edition. September 20, 2024.

Copyright © 2024 Cameron Hart.

ISBN: 979-8227551948

Written by Cameron Hart.

Want a free book?

Sign up for my newsletter[1] and get your free copy of Chasing Stacy!

One look at the stunning waitress carrying the weight of the world on her shoulders, and I'm a goner. I wasn't looking for a sweet little thing with auburn hair and more baggage than I can fit on the back of my bike, but there's no going back now. She's mine. I'll prove to her I'm more than capable of handling her past and making her feel safe again.

---

1. https://dl.bookfunnel.com/7wbqvhsx8r

Chapter 1

Brewer

The ax comes down on the log, splitting it in half with a satisfying snap. I grab the two pieces and toss them on the growing pile next to me. Summer is nearly over, and here on the mountain that means we could be getting the first snow any time now.

I grew up on this mountain, just like my ma and pa, and their parents before them. The only time I left was for college, and even then, I was miserable the whole time until I finally came home. New York City isn't the place for me. I much prefer the pace of mountain life.

However, my father told me the degree in business would be worth it, and he was right. Since returning home, I've had a successful business making custom wooden furniture. It's how I earn an income, though truthfully, I already have everything I need without it. I grow my own food, I helped build the house I currently live in, and the mountain provides me with lush scenery and plenty of activities to take up my time.

Sure, it's a lot of hard labor and long hours in the sun followed by months of harsh winter. And yes, sometimes I miss being able to order a pizza and have it delivered to my door. But if you're able to weather the storms up here in the wilderness of Montana, Wickery Mountain will reward you with food, shelter, and a place to call home.

The mountain has provided everything for me. Ma taught me how to grow everything from squash to spinach, as well as how to cook a mean stew. Pa taught me how to fish and hunt responsibly, respecting mother nature while still taking what we need to survive and live in harmony.

He taught me how to treat a woman, too. He loved my mother with everything in him, and he let her know it every chance he got. Pops always said he had no idea why she chose him, and mom always responded that the mountain brought them together.

I can't believe it's already been five years since her passing. My dad followed her into the afterlife a few short months later. I wasn't surprised.

He always said he couldn't imagine a world without her in it. Still, the loss was devastating.

I've never found a love like that. A love so deep, it transcends life itself. Then again, it's not like I get out much. I only leave the mountain when absolutely necessary, which is about twice a year.

The nearest town is two hours away, but a few large properties surround the base of the mountain, owned by snobby assholes. The people don't even live in their lavish homes most of the time, choosing to visit a few times a year for a getaway into the "wilderness." With their three-story houses and manicured lawns, you could hardly say they're roughing it.

I shake my head as I haul the last of the firewood inside. I know my lifestyle isn't for everyone. It's difficult, sometimes monotonous work, but it keeps me busy. Knowing I have everything I need right here is reward enough. Well, almost everything.

I'm all alone out here since Ma and Pa died. Alone, but not lonely. At least, not until last week. I woke up one morning with an ache in my chest. It felt like someone punched a hole right through me, leaving a void right where my heart used to be.

I've never been more aware of the empty spaces in my cabin, or the cold side of the bed when I roll over in the middle of the night. Never gave much thought to cooking for one and eating at the table by myself, but now it feels heartbreakingly lonely.

The ache has only worsened over the last few days. I've found myself hiking around the mountain in search of... something. All I know is that a piece of me is missing. For some reason, the mountain took a part of me away, but I know it will provide something else to make me whole again. All I have to do is wait and listen.

After stacking the firewood and clearing the yard of splintered wood, I head inside to clean off the day. I have mostly the same routine; shower when I'm done with work, heat up some dinner, and then sit on the porch, listening to nature's lullaby.

A few hours later, I'm in my trusty wooden porch swing that I built for my ma a decade ago. She was beside herself when I finally showed it to her. Now, I sit here at night and replay the sweet moments we had as a family.

My heart squeezes up painfully tight as doubt filters into my thoughts. Will I ever have a family of my own? Someone to love and spoil? Kids to love and raise right?

A twig snaps somewhere to the right of my cabin, pulling me back into the moment. More twigs and leaves rustle and break under the weight of whatever's out there. It's smaller than a bear but too loud to be a wolf or deer. The forest debris crunches under the uneven steps of the animal, getting closer and closer.

My chest grows tight again, so tight it's hard to breathe. *What the fuck?* I've dealt with my fair share of wildlife, but I've never had this reaction before. It's not fear, it's...

Before I can finish my thought, a bright white figure streaks across the clearing of my little cabin and then disappears into the woods on the other side. I'm on my feet, running after it before my brain has a chance to catch up.

It's her.

Who, I'm not sure, but that's the only thought rattling around in my head as I storm after the ethereal figure. I get the feeling she's going to be essential to my survival. I just need to get to her before something else scoops her up.

When I hear a thud and a whimper, I double my speed. It's a woman, alright. And if she's running up the mountain at this time of night, she's probably in trouble. An unfamiliar urgency takes hold of my body, my heart pumping, lungs breathing with one goal in mind: find her and keep her safe.

Sure, I get the occasional naive rich kid wandering up here from time to time, but they mostly stay away for fear of getting lost or, heaven forbid, break a sweat while hiking. Some idiots had a part out here in the woods a few years ago, but I scared the ever-living shit out of them by wearing my bear skin rug as a coat and growling at them from the shadows. Haven't seen any teens up this way since.

I'm still smirking about it when I reach my mystery woman. She's a work of art. Pure and radiant with white-blonde hair that almost matches her white dress. Her fair skin glows as well, almost translucent in the moonlight. I must be making her up. She's too beautiful to be real.

The pressure surrounding my heart is almost unbearable as I look at her. I feel it swelling up in my chest and taking over my entire body. My skin feels too tight and a thin sheen of sweat covers the back of my neck as I raise a trembling hand to my chest. I rub the spot where my heart is trying to break through.

She looks so delicate and out of place, sitting in the middle of a forest in her dress - which I now notice isn't just white, it's a fucking wedding dress. The thought of her belonging to another man makes my skin crawl and my fists clench. I'm ready to snap a motherfucker's neck for touching what's mine.

Mine?

Mine. She's what I've been missing. The mountain brought me an angel. And right now, my angel is scared and needs me to bring her to her new home and make sure she knows she's never leaving my side again.

The beautiful woman gasps, looking off to the left. I follow her gaze and see a mountain lion prowling toward her. Oh, hell no. Not my angel. No fucking way.

The lion roars, making my beautiful woman whimper again and curl up in a ball, trying to make herself as small as possible. Without another thought, I charge the beast, letting out a feral roar of my own.

Chapter 2

Ainsley

I bury my face in my trembling hands, not wanting to see the mountain lion tear me apart limb from limb. I know it's coming. I've heard there were rabid bears up here, but I didn't expect to see a mountain lion. I can hear my mother's voice in the back of my mind, scolding me for my lack of foresight.

I was a fool for running up the mountain, but I couldn't stop myself. I had to escape the impromptu wedding my parents arranged for me. Even thinking those words makes my stomach twist inside out. I knew they were selfish and greedy, but this is on a whole new level. Giving me away like a piece of property? Ambushing me with a wedding? Who the heck has arranged marriages these days? I'm still baffled.

One minute I was staring at my future husband, trying not to cry or throw up, and the next minute, I was off like a bullet. I didn't think, I just ran. I ran away from it all; the unrealistic standards of my parents, my mother's nagging voice, my father's dismissal, the middle-aged man my father promised me to, the guests who had no idea what they were a part of.

I had to get away from everything. A sense of certainty came over me the farther I got from that awful scene. It's my life, and it's time I start living it. My feet carried me to the base of Wickery Mountain and didn't stop until I tripped.

Now that I'm not running, my muscles scream at me, not to mention my wayward feet, which are bare. I didn't have time for a change of shoes before fleeing, and the four-inch monstrosities my mom made me wear were no match for hiking up a mountain. I have a sneaking suspicion that was on purpose. Anything to keep me trapped in a life I didn't ask for.

Why did I come here? I ask myself for the tenth time. Is being eaten alive better than the fate I escaped? Honestly, maybe. I'm equally as terrified of dying the slow death of a cornered, submissive wife, kept in line by any means necessary. And I do mean *any*.

But death by mountain lion will be quick. I hope.

The lion roars, and I know any moment now I'll feel teeth sinking into my skin. Maybe it'll rip my head off first. That would be quick.

A second roar tears through the otherwise quiet night, this one coming from the opposite direction. *Holy crap*. I've never had anyone fight over me before. Go figure it's a battle for which creature gets to devour me.

A feral energy surrounds me, making my heart race, but not just out of fear. Curiosity gets the best of me, and I peer through my fingers just in time to see some sort of large beast charging the mountain lion.

Woah. Looks like it won't be much of a fight after all. In a blur, the unidentifiable creature tackles the mountain lion. They wrestle for a few brief and terrifying seconds. I hear gnashing of teeth and growls, though I'm not sure which beast they're coming from.

There's an agonizing whimper, and then a loud thud, before the mountain lion scrambles up and limps away as quickly as he can. I don't want to look at the creature who could scare off a mountain lion, but I can't seem to close my eyes.

The large figure turns, and I realize it's a man. A *gigantic* man with broad shoulders and dark, messy hair. The moonlight hits him at an angle, casting half of his face into darkness while the other half glows in the silver light. There's a brutal beauty in his fierce eyes. He's untamed. Wild. It makes me want to be wild, too.

My heart thunders in my chest as he approaches me cautiously. I can't tell if he's stalking me so he can pounce or if he's trying not to scare me away. Either way, I can't bring myself to move. It's not just my throbbing head, aching muscles, and raw, torn up feet keeping me in place. It's his eyes. The way they're searching mine, collecting my fears, and drawing out unrecognizable feelings.

He feels like home. Or at least what I want home to feel like. Warm. Safe. Familiar.

Tears sting my eyes, though I don't think it's out of fear. It's like I've missed him my whole life.

The massive man kneels down in front of me, looking me over for damage. His gaze is surprisingly tender as he takes stock of my injuries. It's a stark contrast to his otherwise rough exterior and intimidating size.

"Are you okay, Firefly?" he murmurs.

My heart squeezes up in my chest at his name for me. It seemed to roll off his tongue so naturally. My mystery man waits patiently for my answer, hovering his hands over me without touching me, like he's afraid I'll break.

"Take it easy, now," the man whispers, keeping his distance while still watching my every move. I can't explain why I feel totally safe with him, even though we've only just met.

I open my mouth to say I'm fine, because I'm always fine. Great. My life is blessed and my family is perfect. We do winters in LA and summers in the Hamptons, with the occasional weekend getaway to my father's midlife crisis home in Nowhere, Montana. At least, that's the image I've been forced to project time and time again. If everything looks good on the outside, it must be good all the way through.

Instead of brushing off the stranger's concern and plastering on a smile like I'm supposed to, I shake my head no. Peering into the hazel eyes of my protector, all of my defenses fall away. I don't want to lie to him or feed him the same lines I do everyone else. I want him to know me, the real me.

Maybe that's why I let the tears fall. All of my emotions from the last twenty-four hours rush to the surface, stealing my breath as they push their way out in a broken sob. I'm not even sure what I'm crying about specifically, just that the pain, betrayal, and loss are too much for me to deal with on my own.

God, I'm pathetic. I have nothing, not even shoes. I have no one, not after the stunt I pulled. If I was killed by a mountain lion, not a single person would care. Not really. My parents would be livid that they couldn't manipulate me into marrying up, but no one would mourn me. My meaningless life would have ended, and it would be as if I never existed.

I cry for all of the things I've lost, all the relationships I never had, all the love that was never shown. I cry for the little girl who endured cruel punishments, crash diets, and verbal and emotional abuse. I cry until my temples throb and my throat is sore.

My savior gathers me up in his arms, cradling me to his chest. I'm shocked at first, but that gives way to a sense of safety and acceptance. My automatic response is to cling to him. I want to curl up inside of his warmth and soak up whatever strength he's willing to give me. I don't even notice he's carrying me through the woods until I look around and see a cabin tucked into the corner of a clearing.

"You're okay now, firefly. I'd never hurt you. You're home."

Home. That's what this feels like. I'm home now.

Chapter 3

Brewer

My angel doesn't fight me as I carry her into my cabin. In fact, she sighs so sweetly and relaxes ever so much, melting even more into my embrace. I know she feels it too. She's right where she belongs.

As much as I don't want to set her down, I know I have to clean her up and tuck her into bed so she can rest and recover. I have a million questions, but they'll have to wait. Right now, I need to take care of my woman.

I start to set her down, but she fists my shirt, clinging to me and burying her face into the side of my neck. Fuck, so many emotions slam into me at that simple gesture. She needs me. She wants me. She trusts me to protect her. I don't ever want to let her go, but the sooner I tend to her wounds, the sooner she can be back in my arms.

"I've got you, firefly. I'm not going anywhere," I whisper as I gently set her down on the floor.

She hisses and stumbles backward. I grab her shoulders to steady her, then look her over for any obvious injuries I missed that would make her fall. It's then I notice she's not wearing any shoes. Her delicate feet are all torn up from running barefoot in the woods.

I immediately scoop her back up and head toward the bathroom. I can't imagine what would make her hike up the mountain for nearly three-quarters of a mile without shoes on, but I vow to protect her and make sure she's never put in that position again.

Rolling my shoulders back, I try easing some of the tension in my muscles. Everything in me wants to demand answers, to get the names of every person who is responsible for her cuts and bruises, and break each one of their fingers one by one.

My woman doesn't need to see that side of me right now, though. She needs a warm bath, a warm meal, and a warm bed. There will be time to discuss retribution later, after she's had some rest.

Carefully setting her down on the edge of the tub, I grab a washcloth, wetting it down before kneeling in front of her. She doesn't say anything as I take one of her little feet in my hands and begin gently cleaning up the dirt and cuts littered over her skin. Each one angers me, but I take calming breaths, knowing my firefly needs me to be gentle with her.

After I'm done, I look up into her eyes, which I notice for the first time are light green, almost teal color. Her brow is furrowed and she's chewing on the corner of her lips nervously. She looks between where I'm still holding her foot and my eyes, then takes a deep breath.

"Why are you being so nice to me?"

"Because you're mine." The words are out of my mouth before I can stop them. It's the truth, but I know it might be overwhelming and intense to say to someone after only knowing them for fifteen minutes.

She smiles softly as more tears gather in her eyes. I can't look away from her, and I don't want to. Ever.

"What's your name?" she finally asks. God, her voice. Thick and sweet like honey.

"Brewer."

Her smile turns into a grin, making her teal eyes sparkle. Jesus, I can't breathe. All the blood in my body changes course and heads straight for my dick, which is now throbbing painfully in my jeans.

Down, boy.

I swear the damn thing hasn't risen to the occasion in years, and now he's angry and hard as a fucking rock.

"Brewer," she repeats with a playfulness in her voice that does nothing to help my current condition. "It fits."

I can't help but return her smile, rusty as it may be.

"What's your name?"

"I like Firefly," she whispers.

That hits me deep. If I didn't already know I was keeping her forever, that would have done it. I want to know her real name, of course, but for now, I'm content knowing she likes my name for her. If she wants a new identity, I can give her that. As long as she's mine, I don't give a fuck what her name is.

"Me, too."

We share another lingering look, but then my eyes drop down to her arms, which are covered in little scratches from running through the woods. "Let's get you in the bath, Firefly. You can clean up and relax your muscles. You must be sore."

She nods, but then her brows furrow as she looks at me with anxiety swimming in her beautiful teal eyes. I realize how she might have interpreted my statement. As much as I want to strip her bare and worship her gorgeous body, I also want her to be comfortable and feel safe. It's understandable for her not to want a stranger to see her naked. Though, we're not really strangers, are we?

"I'll start the bath and grab you some of my clothes to change into," I'm quick to follow up. "I'll leave you—"

"No!" she cuts me off. "Please don't leave."

"Never," I assure her, cupping the side of her face. She exhales a breath and practically melts into my arms once again. "I just meant I'd give you some privacy. I'll be right in the kitchen if you need anything.

I give her a gentle squeeze, not wanting to hurt her, and then reach behind her to start the water. I may be a wild mountain man, but this cabin is equipped with plumbing and running water. Ma told my dad she needed to be able to take hot baths without having to heat up water over the fire, and he readily agreed as long as it got her to stay. I've never been more grateful for her stipulation than at this moment.

I help my firefly stand up, knowing her feet have to be killing her. Once she's steady, I turn around and head for the door, intending to give her the privacy I promised her.

"Brewer?" she asks tentatively. "I... could you help me? I can't reach the buttons."

I take a grounding breath and remind myself she's hurt and lost and scared and doesn't need me ogling her. I remind my dick of that too, as he lurches in my pants and dribbles precum.

"Yeah," I croak out.

When I turn around, I see my beautiful woman looking up at me with a bit of nervousness in her eyes. Her anxiety is overshadowed by the trust I see in there as well. I'll make sure she never regrets putting her faith in me.

I step up behind her and sweep her tangled, white-blonde hair over one shoulder so I can undo the twenty or so buttons going down her back. A thought occurs to me as I work on the last button.

"How old are you?" I blurt out. I assume she's at least eighteen if she was getting married today. Fuck, that thought hits me hard as well. "Are you married?"

"No. And I turned nineteen two weeks ago."

Oh, thank fuck.

My firefly giggles, making me realize I said that out loud. I pop open the last button before pushing the straps down her shoulders and letting the tattered dress pool at her feet.

Leaning down, I ghost my lips over her bare shoulder and up the side of her neck. "Good. I don't need to kill anyone then," I whisper into the shell of her ear.

She gasps and looks at me over her shoulder, our faces mere inches apart. *Shit,* that must have sounded possessive and creepy as fuck. I can't help these thoughts, and apparently, I can't contain them, either.

To my complete surprise, she doesn't look afraid of me or my confession. In fact, her teal eyes are wide, almost in awe of my words. "You'd kill for me?"

I nuzzle into the side of her neck and kiss her there, needing to touch and taste her in some way. I'm already obsessed with this woman, but ask me if I give a fuck. "Kill for you. Die for you. Whatever keeps you safe," I promise.

She doesn't respond, and I don't expect her to. I'm sure it will take some time for her to get used to being loved like this. From what I've gathered in our short time together, my angel hasn't had a lot of love in her life.

I help her into the huge clawfoot tub, careful to avoid gawking at her perfect little body. *Soon*, I tell myself. Soon I'll make her mine in every way, but right now she needs a bath and a good night's sleep.

The little angel curls up in the tub, then looks up at me with those big teal eyes. I know what she's going to ask before she even opens her mouth.

"Stay."

Chapter 4

Ainsley

I can't believe I asked him to stay. I mean, who does that? Sure, he rescued me from certain death, and yeah, he's easily the sexiest man I've ever seen, even with his wild hair and calloused hands.

Actually, that only makes him sexier. Everyone my parents paraded me around in front of was stuck-up, repressed, and soft. Bunch of slimy bastards, every last one. The guy I left at the altar was king of the bastards.

But not Brewer. He's untamed, intense, and has me doing things I've never done before. Like letting a stranger strip me down and asking him to stay while I take a bath. His boldness makes me bold. His confidence gives me the confidence to ask for what I want - which is something I was never allowed to do before.

I tuck my knees up and wrap my arms around my legs, suddenly aware of how exposed I am. I've never been completely naked in front of a man before, and I've definitely never initiated something like this. I'm crazy, right? I don't know this man who is looking at me with the most brilliant hazel eyes and dark, messy hair that I want to run my hands through. I want to run my hands everywhere over his hard body and...

No! That's the opposite of what I should be thinking. A massive mountain man just carried me into his home and promptly got me naked within ten minutes of my arrival.

As much as my brain is yelling at me to be wary of my situation, I can't seem to feel anything other than gratitude and curiosity at our profound connection. Out here, I can be anybody. And I want to be *his*.

I see Brewer unbutton his flannel, revealing his bare chest a little bit at a time. It's all I can do not to reach out and demand he let me touch every one of his defined muscles. I have the urge to trace his tattoos with the tip of my tongue and taste his sweat.

What the hell is wrong with me? What is this pressure in my lower belly? Why am I tingly all over? I swallow roughly, unable to figure out why my body is responding to him like this.

Brewer removes his shirt completely, and I automatically turn away from him. It's too much. He's too perfect. Plus, I've never seen a naked man before. When I asked him to stay, I didn't think he was going to get in the tub with me. Would both of us even fit in here?

A deep, rumbling sound comes from Brewer's direction. It takes me a second to realize he's laughing. I get the sense he doesn't do it often. I don't know if he's laughing at me being a prude or not, but I don't care. I'm just happy to hear his laugh.

"Don't worry, Firefly. I'm just taking my shirt off so it doesn't get wet while I wash you."

"Oh," I breathe out, turning my head to look at him once more. I can't help it. Just like my feet that wouldn't stop running up the mountain, my eyes can't stop from finding his when we're apart for too long.

"Unless you just want me to watch?"

"Um..." I know my cheeks are burning bright red. It's one of the unfortunate side effects of having such fair skin. When I blush, I blush hard, and everyone knows I'm either embarrassed, ashamed, or in this case, really turned on. That has to be what the dull ache between my legs is. I've never felt anything like it, but looking at him now, the pressure only gets worse. Almost unbearable.

"Shit, not like that," he rushes to say. "I meant if you didn't want me to touch you, I'd stay while you touched yourself. *Fuck*, that's not... I didn't mean—"

A laugh bubbles out of me as I watch the gruff, sculpted god of a man stammer and get flustered at his own words. He's kind of adorable.

"I know what you meant. I think." I grin at him and wink, feeling flirty for the first time in my life. None of the boys my parents wanted me to marry ever made me feel like being this playful.

Brewer sighs and rubs a hand over the back of his neck as if he's nervous. What does he have to be nervous about? He towers over me, easily a foot taller and a hundred pounds of muscle heavier than me. I'm naked and vulnerable. I'm the one who should be nervous. Instead, I want to put him at ease.

"Thank you for your kindness, Brewer. If you want to, um... if you want to wash me, I wouldn't object."

His eyes snap up to mine, equal parts shock and desire shining through. Slowly, silently, Brewer walks toward the tub and kneels down next to the side, washcloth in hand. He grabs a bar of soap from the sink counter and gets the washcloth soapy before gliding it down my back.

I instantly relax at his touch. Dipping my head down to rest on my knees, I exhale a deep breath. I feel like I'm truly breathing for the first time in so long. As I pull more air into my lungs, the scent from the calming soap he's using fills my head.

"What kind of soap is that?"

Brewer stops rubbing gentle circles on my back. "Do you like it?" he asks, almost tentatively.

"Yeah. It feels so good," I almost moan. Brewer makes some sort of grunting sound in the back of his throat, which makes me giggle. "Where did you get it?"

"I made it."

"No way!" I sit up and turn towards him, realizing all too late that I'm showing him my bare breasts. I lift an arm to cover myself, but when I see Brewer's eyes drift down and settle on my chest, I drop my arm back down. I want him to see me.

Brewer's gaze lingers for a moment longer before he clears his throat and shakes his head as if breaking a trance. "Sage, basil, and lavender. The soap," he stutters out, resuming his gentle washing of my back and shoulders.

He hesitates, and I wonder if he's thinking about washing other parts of me. The crazy thing is... I think I'd let him.

Brewer surprises me by cupping the side of my face in his free hand. "You are the most beautiful woman I've ever seen, angel. But I don't want to take advantage of you or rush you into anything. We have all the time in the world to get to know each other on every level."

"Do we?" The question pops out of my mouth before I can stop it.

Brewer rubs his thumb back and forth over my lips in a featherlight touch, sending shivers throughout my body, landing right in between my legs. This man is driving me crazy, and he's barely even touched me.

"I thought we agreed you were mine," he says softly. There's such tenderness in his voice, it nearly brings me to tears. "I know this is new and overwhelming. I've never felt this way before. I've never had anyone outside of my family here in this cabin, but you belong here. I can't explain it, but you... you're..."

"You too," I whisper. "Whatever I am to you, you are to me. You make me feel..."

"You too." He smiles at me. Brewer leans down and rests his forehead on mine. I feel so safe and protected, surrounded by his strength and gentleness.

Before I can think better of it, I tilt my head up and press my lips against his. We both gasp at the intense sensation that flashes through our bodies. I somehow *feel* his pleasure as much as my own. All of my muscles tense up and the air is stolen from my lungs. Brewer cups the back of my neck and angles my head so he can slide his tongue into my mouth. He gives me the air in his lungs, breathing new life into me with each steady stroke.

"Wow," I whisper once we break apart. My cheeks are flushed, both from what we just did and my stupid remark after.

Brewer brushes his knuckles down one of my cheeks while pressing a soft kiss to my other cheek. "Love seeing your blush, firefly. Love knowing I put it there." He gives me one last lingering kiss and then pulls away from me.

I lean back, resting my head on the back ledge of the tub, exposing my entire body to Brewer's hungry eyes. I watch in fascination as he takes in every inch of me. I want him to look. It belongs to him, after all.

He grabs the washcloth once more, loading it up with more of the soothing soap and dragging it down my chest. He covers one breast with the cloth, the material rubbing against my sensitive nipples. I gasp softly and arch my back at the unexpected jolt of pleasure it sent to my... pussy. I blush even harder just thinking that word. My mom would die if she knew, which makes me want to lean into my newfound freedom all the more.

"You okay?" Brewer asks, halting his movements.

"Feels good," I manage to say. God, is that low, breathy voice really mine?

Brewer grunts and gives my other breast the same attention. This time, my hips buck as I squeeze my thighs together. It's an automatic response to his touch like my body is telling him where I need him most.

The cloth slides down my torso and tummy, getting closer to my throbbing center. Just when I think he's going to touch me there, he changes course and begins washing my ankles and calves, slowly dragging the cloth up, up, up, stopping to rub gentle circles behind one knee and then the other, making my thighs shake. Why do I feel that touch everywhere?

Brewer groans when I spread my legs wider, letting him see all of me.

"So beautiful. My perfect angel," Brewer whispers, his hazel eyes locked on mine.

My entire body aches, my stomach tight and tingly. I've never felt this way before, like every cell is pulsing at once, begging for some sort of relief. I instinctively know Brewer can give me what I'm craving.

I'm about to ask him to touch me, kiss me, do *something* to ease the pressure gathering in my core, but Brewer kisses me on the forehead before whispering, "Let me go get some clothes for you and then I'll feed you and put you to bed."

I can't help but smile at this man in front of me. Even though I'm vibrating with a confusing, frustrating need, I melt at his sweetness and kind words. "Thank you for taking care of me."

"It's my honor to give you everything you need." Brewer gives me one last kiss, and then leaves me to soak in the afterglow of what just happened.

Chapter 5

Brewer

As soon as I close the door to my bedroom, I whip out my cock and stroke the damn thing twice before coming all over my hand.

Holy fucking shit.

My dirty little angel is incredible. The sexiest, sweetest woman in the world somehow ended up on my mountain, in front of my cabin. She trusted me with her precious little body, and soon, I hope she trusts me with her heart.

I've almost convinced myself she isn't real, that this is too perfect to be true. But then I hear my angel sigh and move around in the water, so I know she has to be here. Either that or I've finally lost my mind after being alone up here for so long.

After cleaning myself up and changing my clothes, I grab a shirt and warm socks for my firefly, along with a clean towel. When I get back to the bathroom, I see my woman relaxing in the warm water with a content, happy smile on her face.

She opens her eyes and blushes when she sees me staring at her. I love that fucking blush. It makes me want to bite her red cheeks and kiss away the sting before thrusting my thick dick inside of her virgin pussy.

She didn't have to tell me she's innocent in every way. The way her body responded to my touch, her soft moans, and passionate kisses said it all. She'll be mine in every way, forever. Never thought I was a possessive fucker, but when it comes to Firefly, I'll fight off the whole world to keep her near.

More than the need to be with her physically, I have a desire to hold her and soothe her and make her feel cherished and loved. How I can want both of these things so fiercely at the exact same time is beyond me, but I don't question it. We'll figure it out together.

"Hi," she squeaks out, her blush deepening. So fucking cute.

"Hey, Firefly," I smile at her. Setting the clothes down on the counter of the sink, I step over to the tub and offer my hand to help her up.

I can't keep my eyes off of her body. My angel stands up, water trickling over her perfectly small breasts, curvy hips, and flat stomach. The rivulets trail lower, a few drops catching in the soft curls of her mound.

Fuck me.

I somehow manage to tear my eyes away from the sight before I'm fully hard again.

Handing her the towel, I take a step back and wipe a hand down my face, trying to get my shit together. The little firefly has done a number on me, that's for sure.

As much as I want to throw her naked body over my shoulder and toss her down on my bed, I want to get to know her first. It would kill me if she thought I was only after her body.

"I'm going to warm up some dinner," I finally say, needing some distance between us. "Come out to the kitchen when you're ready."

"Thank you." She smiles sweetly at me.

Once I'm in the kitchen, I take a few deep breaths. I need to get this possessive need to claim her under control. But first I need to feed her and make sure she's on the same page as I am.

I have the stew warming in a pot on the stove when my angel steps into the kitchen. She's wearing one of my sweatshirts that goes down to her knees, along with a pair of wool socks that reach halfway up her toned calves.

We both stare at each other, getting lost in this intense, all-consuming connection we have. One thing's for sure; it's no coincidence my angel is standing here in my kitchen.

She walks toward me, limping slightly. The sight of her in pain feels like a dagger to my chest. I rush over and scoop her up, carrying my woman over to the small dining room table and helping her get situated in the chair.

"That wasn't necessary," she says, rolling her eyes at me. I see a smile and blush, though, so I know she doesn't really mind my overprotectiveness. That's good. I don't think I could stop if I wanted to, and I don't want to.

I shrug and kiss the top of her head, giving her a wink as I head back to grab our dinner. Her eyes go wide when I set the bowl of stew down in front of her.

"What's this?"

"Beef stew." For the first time in my whole life, I feel self-conscious. I still don't know anything about her, but if that fancy wedding dress was any indication, she probably eats fancy meals prepared by professional chefs. And here I am, giving her a bowl of meat and potatoes.

I watch as she lifts the spoon to her mouth and takes her first bite. She chews and thoughtfully considers what she's eating. Finally, she swallows and grins at me before digging in. I let out a huge breath and feel my chest loosen up a bit as my angel devours her food.

"So good," she mumbles around another big bite of stew. Her hand goes up to cover her mouth and her cheeks turn slightly pink. "Sorry. I shouldn't talk with my mouth full."

I can't help the laugh that rumbles through me. "Firefly, that's the joy of living up here on the mountain. No one can tell you what you should or shouldn't do. You're free to make your own choices."

She hits me with a look that nearly has me scooping her up again and holding her to my chest. It's like no one ever told her she's her own person or capable of making her own decisions. The look is gone before I can read any more into it, replaced by a brilliant smile.

"Well in that case..." She sets her spoon down and picks up the bowl, slurping down its contents. It shouldn't make me hard, but fuck if I can help my body's reaction to every little thing she does.

After setting the bowl down, my angel slumps in her chair and pats her belly, a satisfied grin on her face.

"I've never been this full before," she sighs. "It feels good. Like I'm all warm inside." Her eyes widen a bit and that damn blush creeps back into her cheeks. "Uh, that was a weird thing to say," she laughs nervously. "I just meant this was so good. Much better than the rabbit food and diet drinks my mom feeds me all the time," she says, rolling her eyes.

So many thoughts flood my brain. I'm practically beating my chest with pride over the fact I fed my woman something she enjoyed, but I'm pissed that she's never had a solid meal before. Instead of voicing all of that, however, I ask if she wants seconds.

"I can't possibly eat another bite. Seriously, you're going to have to roll me out of here."

"You're not going anywhere," I say a little more harshly than I intended. The thought of her leaving is unacceptable. "I'm keeping you, Firefly."

"Ainsley," she whispers.

"What?"

"My name. It's Ainsley."

"Ainsley," I repeat, rolling it around on my tongue and swallowing it down. "Beautiful."

I get up from my chair and kneel in front of her chair. This woman has literally brought me to my knees more than once in the short time I've known her. I'll stay down here and worship her for as long as she lets me.

Taking her hands in mine, I rub my thumbs over her delicate knuckles and look into her otherworldly teal eyes.

"I'm keeping you, my beautiful Ainsley," I murmur before kissing the back of her hand. She gives me a soft, sweet smile, but then yawns suddenly, making me chuckle. "Let's get you to bed."

She nods and I scoop her up, loving the weight of her in my arms.

"I can walk the five feet to the bedroom," she says, even though she snuggles deeper into my chest.

I wince at the reminder of how my small cabin must look to her. From what I've gathered, Ainsley comes from a family who takes pride in flaunting their money.

"I'll build us a bigger house," I promise as I stand in front of the bed and start to lay her down. She clings to me and nuzzles into my neck. I love when she does that, and I think she knows it too.

"You don't have to do that. I won't take up much space." Ainsley lifts her head up and smiles before kissing my cheek. I turn my head and capture her lips, kissing her properly until we're both out of breath.

"I want more space for you to take up, firefly. I want you to take up every inch of my home, my life, my…" Damn, I almost said my heart. It's true, but I'm already being so intense with my declarations of keeping her forever. "Just, all of me. I want you to fill up every part of me."

My angel kisses my cheek again, and then yawns. I reluctantly set her down and pull the covers over her, kissing my sweet girl on her forehead after I tuck her in. I turn and look around the room, in search of an extra blanket I can take with me to the couch.

"Aren't you coming to bed, too?"

"I can sleep out on the couch. I don't want you to be uncomfortable." The words feel like sandpaper on my tongue.

"Brewer. You've seen me naked and you offered to build me a house. I think you can sleep in bed with me, don't you?"

I can't help but grin at her feistiness. Each new part of her personality she reveals to me only has me falling harder for her. Falling? No. I tripped and landed on my ass right at her feet the moment I saw her.

I strip out of my t-shirt but leave my pants on. I don't miss the hungry look in her eyes as she takes in my bare chest. When she finally looks up at me again, Ainsley licks her lips, making me groan.

She scoots over and pats the space next to her. I don't waste any time crawling in bed and settling in behind her, spooning my body around her much smaller one. I wrap my arms around my perfect firefly and pull her close, holding her while she drifts off to sleep. For the first time in weeks, I fall into a deep, peaceful sleep.

Chapter 6

Ainsley

I can't remember the last time I woke up naturally. Usually, my mornings start with Penny, my maid, dragging me out of bed and getting me dressed for whatever Mom and Dad have scheduled for the day. Every moment of my life has been planned out for as long as I can remember.

Breakfast is at six every morning, then it's off to tutoring until lunch. I either have tennis lessons or piano lessons in the afternoon, usually followed by a fancy dinner with Dad's business partners or a stuffy, boring party. At the end of the day, Penny scrubs off my makeup and peels off whatever awful dress my mom made me wear, and then ushers me into bed so we can start the whole process over again.

Something is different today. Why hasn't Penny snapped at me to get my butt out of bed yet? I roll over and peek an eye open, expecting to see my fluffy white comforter and pink throw pillows. Instead, I see forest green sheets and a thick wool blanket.

And then it hits me.

I'm home.

My true home. With Brewer. This realization has my body going haywire. My heart races, my stomach flips, and my core clenches in a way I've only experienced around my wild mountain man. He told me yesterday the best part about being up here on the mountain is that I can do whatever I want. What if I want to do Brewer?

I can't help the giggle that falls from my lips. I know I'm blushing profusely as well, but I don't care. Brewer said he liked it, which is good. I have a feeling he'll have me blushing all the time.

My beastly yet cuddly Brewer isn't in bed with me, but I'm not worried. I know he's still here. I don't know how, but I feel his presence.

Sitting up, I look around the room for the first time. I didn't get much of a tour yesterday, and honestly, I wasn't up for it. Brewer knew that I needed a bath, some food, and sleep.

I don't know much about cabins or homes or anything like that, but I do know that I love this place. It's an actual log cabin - not the fake log cabin my parents have at the base of the mountain that we visit once or twice a year. That house is a mansion with a "rustic" exterior. Even then, it's not that rustic. Having a fountain on the front lawn doesn't exactly scream *roughing it*.

But Brewer's home is beautiful. Authentic. Lived in. I can feel the love and happy memories in each hand-placed beam. I wonder where his family is. He said last night I'm the only one outside of his family who has been here. I get the sense he's been alone for a while, and that thought has my heart clenching up painfully in my chest. Brewer has so much love to give, and I can't believe I'm here and he seems to want to give it to me.

I'm pretty sure I never want to leave. Brewer talked about keeping me, and I believe him. I just want to make sure he knows I can pull my own weight around here. Granted, my extremely sheltered life didn't teach me much about the real world or how to take care of myself, but I can cook a damn fine meal if I do say so myself.

Despite my mom's many protests, I hung around the kitchen with our chef, Alonzo, as often as I could. He taught me a thing or two before my mom changed my schedule and made it so I never had free time before meals, thus bringing my culinary education to a close. Mother said it was unbecoming of a woman of my status to worry herself with preparing meals. That's what the staff is for. I scoff at the memory of her ridiculousness. She thinks we're royalty, but we're just rich.

The only person who can sympathize is my bestie, Shay. Her family is just as awful as mine, maybe worse. Her mom has been trying to hand Shay off to the most eligible bachelor ever since she turned sixteen. Even with the awful, traumatic attack last year, her parents won't ease up on playing matchmaker.

Shay is the one person I'll miss from my old life.

Frowning, I decide to find a way to reach her. Maybe I can convince her to leave her awful family in Seattle and move out here to Montana with me.

With that thought in mind, I stretch and hop out of bed, noting that I feel a lot better than I did last night. I'm still sore, but on the whole, I feel like a new person in more ways than one.

Making my way to the kitchen, I'm almost giddy with excitement at cooking for my Brewer. I look in the cupboards and small fridge to see what I have to work with. There's a bowl of eggs in the fridge, which is an odd way to store them, but whatever. I grab the eggs and set them on the counter next to a loaf of bread I found. I dig around in the cupboards for some seasonings and find little jars of herbs and spices, each with a hand-written label. I'll have to ask Brewer about that later.

Surveying my available ingredients, I get to work making tomato basil garlic scrambled eggs and toast. The back door swings open right as I'm plating our food. I hear Brewer's heavy footsteps grow louder until he's standing mere inches from me, shirtless and sweaty.

Suddenly, I'm not hungry for breakfast at all.

"Firefly."

"Brewer."

It's the only word I get out before his lips crash down on mine. I taste his salty sweat on my tongue, mixed with his natural flavor. I moan and drink down more of him, needing it all.

Just as quickly as it started, the kiss ends.

"I really like seeing you in my kitchen, angel," he says, still holding me in his arms and smiling down at me.

"Well, I really like being in your kitchen," I tell him with a grin. He's looking at me like I'm the love of his life. I'm sure I'm looking at him the exact same way. "Where were you?"

"Out checking the traps and feeding the animals."

"Animals?!" I ask excitedly.

"Yeah," he chuckles, giving me another kiss. "I'll give you the full tour after breakfast. I'll devour the food you made, and then I'll devour you."

"Uh, me?" I squeak out.

"Yeah, beautiful," he murmurs, nuzzling into my neck and kissing a trail up to the shell of my ear. "I'm going to have my mouth on every fucking inch of your body." I feel Brewer's big hands slide underneath the sweatshirt I'm wearing, trailing up my thighs and gripping my hips. He pulls me close, making me whimper. "But first, breakfast."

I gasp when he steps away from me, which only makes him chuckle. Recovering quickly, I turn to our plates and set them down on the table, motioning for Brewer to join me.

"Holy shit, Firefly, these eggs are amazing," he says around a mouthful of food.

"Thank you," I whisper, beaming at his praise. I stare at him eating for a beat too long before realizing I'm being a creeper. "Why do you call me Firefly?" I ask, hoping to distract myself from the bare-chested, muscled god sitting across the table from me.

Brewer looks up at me with a warm smile that makes the green in his hazel eyes stand out more. "I saw you run right by my cabin with your light hair, fair skin, and white dress glowing in the moonlight. Everything about you lit up the dark forest. That's when I knew I had to have you for my own."

I smile at him, but inside my gut twists remembering that damn wedding dress. As if sensing my thoughts, Brewer sets his fork down and takes my hand in his, rubbing gentle circles over my knuckles.

"Do you want to tell me why you were in a wedding dress?" he asks softly.

I sigh and shake my head no, and then yes. "I suppose I should, huh?"

"What did I tell you about living up on the mountain, firefly? No one is here to tell you what you should or shouldn't do. I'd like to know more about you, everything about you, really, but only if you want that, too. I can be patient as long as you know you're mine."

I'm out of my chair and crawling into Brewer's lap before I even realize what I'm doing. He doesn't miss a beat. His arms wrap around me and he holds me close against his warm, chiseled chest. I bury my face in Brewer's neck, loving the way he sighs and relaxes when I kiss him there. I gather my thoughts while breathing in his manly scent of earth and pine and sweat.

I don't even know where to start, but the words come spilling out of me, almost without my permission. I tell him about growing up in a large estate in Seattle, how my parents pretty much kept me locked up unless they needed to parade me around for a party or to keep up appearances of a happy family.

I tell him about visiting the property we own up here once a year, and how I tend to wander off into the woods or out to the nearby lake, only to get in trouble for being unladylike and ruining my complexion by getting too much sun.

He holds me and whispers reassuring things while I lay everything out before him, letting him know what he's getting himself into by claiming me as his own.

"And then two weeks ago, we came up here for my nineteenth birthday," I say after taking a deep breath. I haven't even gotten to the wedding dress part yet, but Brewer doesn't seem to mind.

"Two weeks ago. Huh," he says to himself. I give him a curious look and he just grins and kisses the tip of my nose. "I woke up one morning a few weeks ago with an ache in my chest. It got worse every day until the mountain delivered you to me."

My eyes fill with tears, and he wipes them away, kissing my forehead and breathing me in. "When I escaped, my feet carried me up the mountain. I couldn't stop running. It felt like I was being pulled, like I knew something was out here, waiting for me."

"Not something, Firefly. Some*one*. I was waiting for you." I nod and rest my forehead on his. "Now, can you tell me why you ran? What did you need to escape?"

"My parents had been talking about finding a suitable husband for me that would strengthen their business partnerships. They were showing me off at parties, not even trying to hide the fact that they were selling me to the highest bidder. I hate their money. I hate what it did to them. I never want to live like them, Brewer. I never want the kind of wealth they have."

He tenses. Did I say something wrong? Eventually, Brewer relaxes. "No one will ever treat you that way again, angel. No one will touch what's mine."

"No one," I agree, kissing the stubble on his jaw. Brewer grunts and tips his head down to capture my lips with his. The kiss is demanding, territorial, and yet tender.

"What happened next?" he asks once we break apart.

"We were having a big birthday party yesterday. My parents had the whole thing planned out, like always. All I had to do was put on a dress and play the part they wanted me to. I thought it was going to be another boring soiree, an excuse to rub shoulders with the elite under the guise of celebrating my birthday. But my maid, Penny, and my mom came into my room yesterday and dressed me in that gown, telling me it's my duty and how my marriage is going to secure lots of business deals and make our family very powerful."

"Oh, Ainsley..." Brewer whispers, stroking my back.

"I was outside, right before the ceremony. I remember hiding behind the stupid fountain in our yard, holding my bouquet with trembling hands. I watched my dad shake hands with a large, older man, who I recognized from some of the parties we went to. He's probably in his fifties, I think he's been married three times before. I thought he was the father of the groom, but then I saw him take his position up on the makeshift stage next to the priest."

"Fuck," Brewer grumbles.

"Yeah," I laugh bitterly. "I thought the same thing. So, I ran. I dropped my flowers, kicked off my shoes, hiked up my dress, and fled. Like I said, my feet knew where they were going," I say with a shrug.

Brewer doesn't say anything for a few agonizing moments, but then he stands up with me in his arms, and walks over to the couch. Once we're settled with me straddling his lap, Brewer cups my face in his hands and just stares at me. I watch his beautiful eyes study my face like he wants to memorize everything about me.

"I'm so sorry your parents didn't love you the way you deserve. So fucking sorry. I don't know why the mountain found me worthy to take care of you, but I swear I will protect, cherish, and love you with every breath and beat of my heart."

He wipes away my tears and rests his forehead on mine. "Love?" I whisper.

Brewer leans back and tucks my hair behind my ear. "Love," he confirms. "I love you, little firefly. I've long stopped questioning the wisdom of the mountain and started accepting the gifts it's given me. And you, Ainsley, are the greatest gift I could have ever asked for."

"I love you too, Brewer. I don't know how it happened so fast, but..."

"But it's true. It's real. I feel it. I feel you. Now let me show you. Let me show you I'll love you always, money or no money." I don't have a chance to ask what he means before I find myself lying on my back on the couch, with Brewer towering over me. His hazel eyes lock onto mine and stare down into the very core of who I am. He looks like he wants to say something, maybe confess something, but instead, he kisses my forehead and whispers, "Do you trust me, my beautiful angel?"

Chapter 7

Brewer

My entire body vibrates with the need to sink ten inches deep into Ainsley's snug little pussy, but she's not ready for that yet. I can give her other pleasures though.

I hover over my angel, holding myself up with a hand on either side of her head, my muscles tense and shaking as I wait for her answer. Staring into her mesmerizing blue-green eyes, I'm shocked and humbled by the emotions I find. There's so much I want to tell her, that I *need* to tell her, but I can't seem to find the words.

I knew Ainsley was it for me the moment I saw her, and each subsequent moment has only made me love her more. Looking at her now, I know without a doubt she feels the same way. This incredible woman loves me as much as I love her. Just like that, our bond is formed; absolute and unbreakable.

"I trust you, Brewer. I trust you with everything. All of me. I'm yours."

My dick throbs painfully in my jeans, but it's my heart that has me gasping for air. I didn't think it was possible, but I somehow love her more. Like she opened up parts of my soul I didn't know were there, just so she could fill them and make me complete in a way I never knew existed.

I lean down and kiss Ainsley's forehead, her button nose, her rosy cheeks, and finally, her sexy little mouth. I drink from her lips, sipping at first with teasing kisses and then diving in, drowning in her and giving her everything right back.

Ainsley spreads her legs to accommodate my large frame, allowing me to settle my hips between her thighs and rub my erection against her center. Jesus, she's not wearing any underwear. I groan when I feel her warm juices seep into my jeans, teasing my cock with a hint of her sweet heat.

"Oh," Ainsley gasps softly. "*Ohhhh* my God..."

I kiss down her neck and smile into her shoulder as she grinds her cunt against me. My dirty angel will only ever know pleasure by *my* hand, *my* tongue, *my* dick. Goddamn. I'm a mountain man, not a caveman, but I fucking love knowing her body belongs to me and only me.

"Ready for more, beautiful?"

"Yes, please," she sighs.

I grin and kiss her again, pulling her bottom lip through my teeth. "So polite, Firefly. I'm going to have to break you of that. There's no one to impress out here, love. Just me."

"What if I want to impress you?" Her cheeks burn bright red like she's embarrassed, but it's the fire in her eyes that lets me know she means every word.

"You want to impress me? Spread your legs wider, baby. Let me get a closer look at what's mine."

Ainsley whimpers, the sound so sweet and filthy in my ears. Her legs fall open, allowing me to scoot down the couch until I'm staring at her drenched pussy. Christ, she's breathtaking.

Without wasting another second, I guide one of her legs over the back of the couch, opening her up even more for my greedy eyes. I massage her inner thighs, rubbing soft circles with my thumbs, up, up, up, closer to her center, loving the way she's already trembling for me.

I spread her pussy lips with my thumbs, revealing her hard little clit, just begging for attention.

"Um, Brewer?" Ainsley asks tentatively. It takes every single ounce of strength to tear my eyes away from her naked form, but I never want her to be uncomfortable, especially when we're together like this.

"Yeah?" It comes out more like a growl instead of a question from a concerned lover, but fuck, this girl has me busting apart at the seams - in more ways than one.

"It looks like you're going to..."

I didn't think her face could get any redder, but she's nearly scarlet.

"Say it," I grunt, sniffing her pussy while keeping my eyes on hers. I can't help it. I'm desperate for a hit, desperate to finally taste her sweet honey. I'm nearly feral with the thought of being covered in her cream, but I'll wait until she gives me permission, even if it kills me.

"It looks like you're going to... put your mouth on me down, um, down *there*," she whispers.

I nuzzle into her mound, burying my nose in her soft curls and growling into her core. Her thighs tremble and I fucking *smell* her arousal as it builds and spills out of her.

"That's exactly what I'm going to do. I'm going to make you come on my tongue, and you're going to love it. You're going to beg me for it. And I'll give it to you every damn time, angel."

"Oh. Okay then," she breathes out.

I chuckle at her response. Still so damn polite. I'm going to have so much fun getting her out of her shell and making her my filthy fucking angel.

I place a kiss over her mound, part her lips with my thumbs once again, and take my first taste. I flatten my tongue and slowly lick up her slit, taking time to cover every inch I can before swirling the tip of my tongue over her clit.

Ainsley jerks and cries out, clawing at the couch while I suck on her little bundle of nerves. I'm relentless in my pursuit of her orgasm, calling it forth and bringing it right to the surface before backing off.

"What? Why did you stop?" she pants. Ainsley fists my hair and tries to shove me back down, which makes me grin.

"Feel good?" I smirk, licking her cream off of my lips.

"You know it does," she says exasperatedly.

I lean up and kiss her briefly, letting her taste herself on my tongue. She moans and slides her hand down my back digging her nails into my skin. I growl and deepen our kiss, slipping my hand in between us to circle her clit with my fingers while I fuck her mouth with my tongue.

Ainsley gasps and moans into my mouth as I build her back up, but I don't let her come up for air. Each time she pulls away from me, I follow her, locking my lips on hers and drawing her into another kiss.

I rub a gentle circle over her entrance, groaning when I feel her little hole pulse for me. Slowly, I push the tip of my finger inside, both of us gasping at how fucking *tight* she is.

"Jesus," I mutter, working my way inside of her with gentle thrusts of my finger while keeping her clit stimulated with my thumb.

"Brewer, Brewer, oh God, I've never..."

Her innocence snaps the last thread of control I had. I thrust my finger inside of her in quick, brutal bursts and press my thumb down on her bundle of nerves. She whimpers as I fingerfuck her hard and fast.

"I know, baby. Take it all. That's it. So beautiful for me."

I curl my finger up and tap that secret spot. Her breath catches in her throat and her back bows off the couch. I kiss her neck and then sink my teeth into her flesh right as she falls apart for me.

Ainsley yelps and grunts out her orgasm, her guttural sounds making me ache with need for her. I drop down between her legs once again, lapping up her release as it pours out of her. She twists, trying to get away from me as her pleasure overwhelms her, but I grip her hips and keep devouring her, just like I promised I would.

Incredibly, her legs snap around my head and begin shaking uncontrollably. I know she's about to come again, and fuck, it might just send me over the edge, too.

I double my efforts, licking and sucking her folds even as she continues to thrash and cry out from her first orgasm. I grind my hips against the couch seeking some sort of relief for my dick. Her whimpers turn to cries, which give way to an earth-shattering scream.

My angel thrusts her pussy into my face as she squirts all over me. I suck her juices down and growl into her convulsing cunt as I hump the damn couch for some relief. It feels like we've been here in this moment of ecstasy for so damn long, and yet it's over too soon. I know I'll never get enough of her.

Ainsley drops back down onto the couch as a sleepy smile spreads across her flushed face. I give her pussy one last kiss before sitting up and pulling her into my lap. I know we need to clean up eventually, but right now, we need this. She snuggles into my chest as I wrap my arms around her and kiss the top of her head.

I don't know how long we stay like that, but eventually, Ainsley pops her head up and gives me the biggest smile I've ever seen. I'm so caught up in memorizing every single thing about her sparkling eyes and wide smile, I miss the question she asked.

"Brewer?" she prompts, lifting an eyebrow and giving me a cheeky little grin like she knew exactly what I was doing. I kiss her nose and wink at her.

"Yeah, Firefly?"

"Could we go on that tour now? I've always loved animals. I asked for a pet every year for my birthday and Christmas for as long as I can remember, but mom said they were dirty and—"

"Unladylike?" I finish for her. She nods. "Fuck that. You can have whatever you want. Let me show you the farm animals I have, and you tell me what else you'd like."

Her teal eyes search mine in disbelief. "Really?"

"Absolutely. Without question. I'd give you the world, Ainsley." And I would. Truthfully, I really could get her anything she could ever want. But I don't know how she'll take that news. She wants nothing to do with wealth or money. I just hope she knows she's it for me, no matter what. I'd give up everything for her.

My firefly grins and kisses my cheek before hopping off of my lap. I grip her hips and pull her back down, cupping her face and kissing her properly. No way I'm letting her get away with a little peck on the cheek. When we break apart, Ainsley smiles and sighs so sweetly before waltzing away toward the bathroom.

Twenty minutes later, we've both cleaned up a bit and changed our clothes. Ainsley is in another oversized shirt of mine, matched with another set of equally as oversized socks that crawl halfway up her legs.

She doesn't have anything else aside from her tattered wedding gown, but it's been crumpled in the corner of the bathroom since last night. Neither one of us seems to want to even look at it, let alone touch it. I hate the thought of her walking down the aisle to another man. Thankfully, she didn't. In fact, she ran in the opposite direction, right up the mountain and into my arms.

I lace my fingers in hers while we walk to the pens I have set up on the east side of my property. Tugging her into my side, I wrap my arm around her shoulders and kiss the top of her head. Ainsley stumbles a bit in the pair of boots I set her up with. They are comically large on her otherwise small frame, but there's no denying how fucking cute she is, drowning in my clothes.

I scoop her up, loving when she giggles and kisses the side of my neck. I carry her the rest of the way to the chicken coop, setting her down once we're inside.

"Oh wow! They are so beautiful!" she exclaims. "Is this why the eggs were in a bowl in the fridge instead of a carton?"

"Yup. Fresh eggs every morning. No store-bought stuff here, if I can help it."

Ainsley turns and looks at me over her shoulder with the softest smile on her lips. Her teal eyes sparkle with something close to adoration. I'll spend every second of every day getting her to look at me like that again.

"That's amazing," she says softly, beaming at me with excitement. "Is that why the spice jars were all labeled by hand? Do you grow everything yourself?"

I nod, swallowing around the lump of emotion in my throat. Knowing my woman approves makes me so damn proud of the work I've done. I realize now it was all for her. I take her hand in mine and squeeze her delicate fingers.

"Want to see?"

She nods enthusiastically, and fuck, I feel like my heart might burst with happiness.

We wander around my property - *our* property - for the next few hours. I show her the greenhouse where I grow all kinds of herbs, vegetables, and some fruit. She's so excited about every new thing she sees, asking questions, and even requesting a few things she'd like to see in the future so she can make certain dishes. Damn, hearing her plan for the future is every-fucking-thing to me.

After visiting the sheep and lone dairy cow, Ainsley yawns and stretches, her arms reaching up to the sky as she bows her back. The hem of the shirt she's wearing rides up, making me bite back a groan. When she looks at me with a naughty, mischievous little twinkle in her eye, all bets are off.

Ainsley is slung over my shoulder in the next second as I storm back to the house. Her giggles fill the air, as well as my soul. I love this woman with everything I am. I close my eyes and thank the mountain for trusting her to my care.

"Where are we going?" she asks, smacking my ass playfully. I reciprocate, spanking her perky little cheeks. Ainsley laughs again and then relaxes in my hold.

"I've got plans for you, firefly."

"Oh yeah?" Her once playful voice is now deeper, almost sultry. She's so damn sexy without even trying.

"Fuck yeah," I growl.

"Well, hurry up then!"

I bark out a laugh and then spank her harder, groaning when she gasps and wiggles.

"Whatever you say, angel." With that, I jog the rest of the way to the cabin, my precious cargo in tow.

Chapter 8

Ainsley

Brewer carries me to the bedroom and tosses me down on the mattress before falling on top of me and fusing his mouth to mine. He dominates this kiss, tangling his tongue with mine and owning me with each demanding stroke.

I love feeling his weight on top of me, pressing me down and pinning me in place. I spread my legs for him, but my movement is halted when I accidentally kick him with my boot. Brewer pulls away from me and chuckles breathlessly, resting his forehead on mine as we recover.

"Guess I forgot to get you undressed, huh?" he says, kissing his way down my neck.

I nod, still not able to form words yet. My skin hums with awareness of every place he's touching me. Brewer pops open the first button on the shirt I'm wearing, placing a kiss over the exposed skin. He continues unbuttoning the shirt and kissing down my chest and torso, finally spreading the material open so I'm bare before him.

Brewer slides off the bed, sinking to his knees and taking off one boot and then the other. He massages my feet so tenderly while giving me a fierce look. The combination of his sweet touch and feral eyes has me twisting in his grip, trying to relieve the ache threatening to take over my body.

Sensing my need, he grips my thighs in his massive hands and pries my legs apart. I cry out and bow my back off the bed when Brewer presses his thumb over my clit. A sudden powerful burst of pleasure slices through me and rattles me to my core.

Before I can recover, his tongue is on my dripping wet cunt, licking me and nipping at my sensitive flesh. He nudges my clit with his nose and then spears his tongue into my little hole, scooping out my juices and drinking them down.

Then I feel him drag his tongue lower, lower, lower, until it's teasing my back entrance. I gasp at the filthiness of it all, but the forbidden nature makes me even wetter. He licks around the tight ring of muscles and growls.

"Holy fuck," I whisper. "Holy fuck, fuck, fuck," my whisper turning into a loud moan when the very tip of his tongue pushes inside. Brewer rubs my clit in furious circles, and I grip the sheets, twisting them in my fists as my body expands and contracts. "Brewer, I'm…"

I shatter before I even finish my sentence. My orgasm rushes through me with such intensity, I shoot up off the bed, trying to escape the overwhelming pleasure. Brewer shoves me back down with a hand spread out over my stomach. He holds me there, making me feel all of it, every last drop of bliss.

I lay on the bed, an absolute puddle. I'm vaguely aware of Brewer standing up and tearing his clothes off. When he doesn't return to me right away, I manage to sit up on my elbows, though it takes considerable effort. I pry my eyes open and see him standing in front of me, pinching the head of his cock as he tilts his head back and takes a deep breath.

"Are you okay?" I ask.

"Yeah," he grits out. "Trying not to come right now."

"Oh. But I haven't even touched you…"

"You don't have to touch me to make me delirious with desire, angel. Every fucking thing you do turns me on, but watching you come…" He groans and strokes his dick. I finally get a good look at it, and my jaw drops open. "You gotta stop looking at me like that."

I barely register his words, mesmerized by the white drops of liquid steadily pouring from the tip of his cock. Suddenly I want to taste him like he's tasted me twice now.

Brewer squeezes his eyes shut as his entire body shakes. I slip off of the bed and sink to my knees in front of him. I have no idea what I'm doing, I just know I need to run my tongue over his hard length. Leaning forward, I lick up the drop of pearly liquid from his tip, gasping as the salty flavor hits my tongue.

"Ainsley! Jesus, woman, what are you doing?"

He sounds angry. I sit back on my heels and look up at him. Brewer's hazel eyes are nearly black as they stare right through me.

"Did I do it wrong? I wanted to taste you like you tasted me."

"You're going to be the death of me, my sexy fucking angel. Don't stop now, love. Anything you do will feel amazing. It's all for you, Ainsley. All for you."

His words make me bold. I replace his hand with mine, gripping the base of his cock. I give him a few strokes like he was doing, testing out what he likes. Brewer hisses out a breath when I squeeze him harder. Tightening my grip, I begin pumping in a steady rhythm while parting my lips and taking the head of his shaft into my mouth.

Brewer mutters a string of curses under his breath and weaves his fingers in my hair, pulling it back into a ponytail. He tugs at the strands and I look up at him, his dick still halfway in my mouth.

"So goddamn beautiful, Firefly. So perfect, sucking my cock like a good girl."

I feel myself blush at his praise, and I continue taking him deeper while jerking off the base of his cock that won't fit in my mouth. He grunts and bucks his hips, stuffing me so damn full of him. I love it. I crave it.

"Shit," he growls. Brewer yanks my head back by my hair and lifts me up before guiding me toward the bed. His hands skim down the sides of my body almost reverently, and then he pushes me backward, my back landing on the soft mattress. "Need to be inside you when I come," he grunts.

I nod my head and spread my legs for him, inviting him to do just that. "I want that too," I whisper.

Brewer climbs up my body and crashes his mouth down on mine in a passionate kiss. "How is every single thing you say the hottest goddamn thing?" He doesn't give me a chance to answer before his tongue is in my mouth again.

Leaning back slightly, he gathers my hands and guides them over my head. He pins my wrists down with one of his massive hands and grips his dick with the other one. Brewer drags his cock through my folds, coating himself in my cream before lining up with my entrance.

"Ready for me? For us? For forever?" His voice is soft, tender, and genuine. I see him struggling to hold back, and yet I know he'd stop at any time if I asked him. But I don't want him to stop. Not now, not ever.

"I want it all. I'm ready, Brewer."

He kisses me as he thrusts all the way inside, tearing through my innocence and finally claiming me as his own. "I'm yours," I whisper. I hadn't meant to say the words out loud, but the look on Brewer's face lets me know he loves it.

"Yes the fuck you are, Firefly," he grunts, hitting all the way home. He stretches me out, molding me to fit him and only him.

His thickness scrapes along my walls, the friction like striking a match as instant, overwhelming heat engulfs me. My stomach flips and spins, bliss pumping through my veins instead of blood.

"Christ, tell me you're okay, angel," he grits out, the pain of holding back evident in his voice. Brewer slides the hand holding my wrists down my arm and cups my cheek, brushing his thumb across my blush. His eyes capture mine, waiting patiently, *painfully*, for my response.

"I'm so good," I murmur. "More, Brewer. More, more, more," I moan, clenching my pussy around him.

He growls and kisses me, pulling my leg higher up on his hip, changing the angle. His cock slides against some magical place inside me that has me sobbing his name louder with each thrust. Brewer snaps his hips against mine, grinding his pelvis against my clit while hammering into that special spot.

Brewer grunts my name every time his balls slap against my ass. I can feel him losing control, his strokes becoming deeper, harder, so damn rough. I love it. I claw at his arms and thrash beneath him, throwing my head back as I cry out his name over and over.

I convulse as he thrusts into me relentlessly. The exquisite pleasure bordering on pain builds and builds, higher and higher, one more, one more, again, again... until I break. Shards of pleasure cut me and heal me as I scream his name.

My orgasm rips through me, holding my body hostage, forcing me to feel every wave of bliss until tears drip down my face and I'm a sweaty, soaking mess beneath him.

One minute I'm clenching around his cock, and the next minute I'm empty. Bereft. I whimper at the loss of him, but he doesn't leave me aching for long.

"I've got you." Brewer's voice is deep and dark, sending fire dancing along my nerves.

I feel his large hands grip my hips, and then I'm flipped onto my stomach. Brewer pulls my hips back, getting me in position on my hands and knees. He runs his hands up and down my back, and then he squeezes my ass cheeks in a punishing hold, spreading them apart and exposing every inch of me.

He slams into me on a growl, and I brace myself for the hard and fast way he's fucking me.

"Oh, God, Brewer, it's, it's... you're so deep," I moan, pushing back against him as he thrusts forward. Each gut-twisting stroke winds me up higher and higher, until I'm right on the precipice, teetering on the edge.

His hips stutter as he loses his rhythm and starts rutting into me. His fingers dig into my hips as my fingers dig into the mattress, both of us clinging on to this tension-filled pleasure. A shiver runs through me, followed by another and another until I'm shaking violently.

My arms give out and Brewer collapses on top of me, wedging his cock impossibly deeper as he grinds into my pussy. I feel his lips on my neck, and then his teeth as he bites down, releasing all the pressure in one massive explosion.

We both cry out as his hot seed spills into me. Wave after wave of his cum splashes into my cunt and then drips out, and still, there's more. My pussy snaps around him as I sob out my climax.

I'm gasping for air as I float back down to Earth, the oxygen burning my lungs and yet somehow sending jolts of pleasure to my clit. Brewer nuzzles into the side of my neck where he bit me, kissing the mark I'm sure he left behind.

Neither one of us moves, but I don't mind. He's holding himself up by his forearms so he doesn't crush me completely, but part of me wishes he would. I want to dissolve into him, this beastly man who saved me, cleaned me up, took care of me, and now loves me with all of his heart. I feel it. I love him, too. So damn much.

Eventually, Brewer pulls out of me, both of us groaning at the loss. He rolls onto his back and drapes me across his chest, getting us as close as possible. Brewer cups my cheek and kisses my forehead so sweetly before kissing one tear-stained cheek and then the other.

"Are you okay, firefly? Jesus, I fucked you so damn hard."

I scoot up and kiss his nose, smiling sleepily at my wild mountain man. "And I loved every second."

His eyes flash with fierce desire before softening. "Me, too, Ainsley," he murmurs before tucking me into his chest. I sigh contentedly and curl up into his warmth, loving the safety I find there. "Rest now, my little angel."

Brewer rubs calming circles on my back, and I melt even more into him as sleep takes me under. My last thought is how this is the happiest I've ever been.

Chapter 9

Brewer

I love everything about waking up with Ainsley in my arms. Love the way her hair spreads out over the pillow, the white-blonde strands sparkling in the early morning light. Love her warm, soft little body pressed against mine. I love each and every steady breath she takes, knowing they give her life and sustain her. I hope she knows I'll do the same. I'll be her everything.

Ainsley stirs slightly, her ass pressing up against my morning wood. I bite back a groan but can't stop my hand from sliding down her torso and cupping her bare pussy. This time I can't hold in my groan. She's fucking *drenched* for me. My dirty little angel must be having some good dreams.

She sighs so sweetly and grinds into me as I massage her little bundle of nerves. Ainsley moans softly, though I don't think she's awake yet. My lips find the side of her neck, and I kiss her there, breathing her in.

I dip one finger into her entrance, and then two, slowly thrusting in and out, massaging her walls as I grind the heel of my palm into her clit. Ainsley gasps and tenses in my arms, and I know she's awake.

"Brewer..." she cries out, bucking her hips and taking more of me. She raises her arm over her head and tangles her fingers in my hair, pulling me down and urging me to kiss her neck. I gladly do, licking and nipping at her sensitive skin. "So good..."

I growl at her sexy, needy little whimper and guide her top leg over mine. I wedge my aching cock in between her ass cheeks, seeking some relief but not entering her. "What were you dreaming about, firefly? You were so fucking wet for me, I couldn't resist."

"I-I... I dreamed..." she gasps as a wave of her arousal gushes over my fingers, still buried deep inside of her swollen channel. "Y-you were..."

I withdraw my hand and smack her clit, just hard enough to sting. Her broken cry and pulsing pussy let me know she likes a little pain with her pleasure. "Tell me," I grunt, caging her clit in with a finger on either side. I rub up and down, keeping her aching for me, but not touching her where she needs me most.

"Oh God, please...please *fuck* me," she whines, her whole body shaking with desire.

I chuckle at hearing her swear word. My angel is as sweet and polite as they come, but I'm teaching her to let go of her old life and embrace life with me. "Tell me what you were dreaming about. I'll remind you every day that you can be whoever you want to be up here on the mountain. I know you want to be my filthy angel, so tell me. Tell me about your dream and I'll make it come true."

"You were... making love to me," she says softly. It's not what I was expecting, but I love that she's opening up to me. "Slowly, at first. I felt... cherished."

"You are, Firefly," I whisper into the shell of her ear before kissing the sensitive spot underneath it. I begin pumping my fingers in and out of her, slowly, just like she's describing. "What else, love?"

"You picked up your speed, but still took your time, driving me insane," she murmurs.

"Like this?" I ask, thrusting into her faster as I place open-mouthed kisses over her shoulder.

"Yes," Ainsley moans. "You went faster with each thrust like you couldn't control yourself."

"I can't," I grunt, adding a third finger and fucking her hard and fast. I curl my fingers up and tap her G-spot over and over. Ainsley tightens her hold on my hair, tugging at the strands to the point of pain. I fucking love it.

She's so close, so goddamn close. Her cream drips out of her as she writhes in my arms. I hold her there, keeping her orgasm just beneath the surface. I feel it claw at her insides, making her whimper with each breath.

Right before it hits, I take my hand away, moving it to her ass and spreading her cheeks. Without warning, I line up to her entrance and push her over the edge with one long, powerful thrust. She fucking falls headfirst into her climax, screaming my name and soaking my dick with her release.

I hold still inside of her, growling as I feel her orgasm ripple around my cock. Before she has a chance to recover, I begin hammering into her, setting a relentless pace. I grip her breast roughly, using them as leverage to fuck into her harder, hitting her so damn deep with each stroke.

"B-Brewer... Brewer, fuck, fuck, fuck yes," she chants over and over. I drop my hand from her breast and blur my fingers over her clit until her pussy clenches around me and soaks me with another orgasm.

I pull out and flip her on her back, wrenching her legs apart and slamming home. Her back bows off the bed and her legs wrap around me, holding me close. She digs her heels into my ass and claws my back, leaving her mark on me.

"Jesus, fuck," I snarl, before claiming her lips as my own.

I devour her, biting at her lips and spearing my tongue inside of her eager mouth, licking up every inch and then sucking on her tongue. It's a wild, messy kiss, one that matches the way I'm fucking her like a goddamn animal.

I slide one hand down her body and grip her ass cheek, changing the angle of her hips and helping her meet me thrust for thrust. My cock scrapes against her most sensitive spot with each fierce stroke.

She's breaking apart for me; I can feel it. Every time I hit the end of her, she cracks a little more, the pressure of her orgasm building and pulsing and pushing her boundaries.

My balls draw up tight as my own orgasm gathers in the base of my spine. My rhythm falters slightly as I try to hold on, needing her to come with me. "Get there, angel, fuck, please get there. Need one more from you."

"It's too much, too much..."

"I've got you, Firefly. Let go for me, I'm right here. Let go, love."

She sucks in a huge breath and holds it, her whole body trembling and then freezing. Every damn muscle is pulled so tight as she clings to me with everything she has. With one last brutal thrust, we both shatter completely.

Ainsley floods my cock with her release, and I give her everything in return, my cum splashing into her throbbing pussy as she sucks down every last drop. We're both grunting, shaking, sweating as we ride that high together.

Eventually, Ainsley goes limp in my arms. I bury my face into the side of her neck and pump into her twice more before collapsing. I roll to the side and drape my freshly fucked little angel over my chest.

Cupping the side of her face, I tip her head up and kiss her closed eyelids and flushed cheeks. She gasps and blinks her eyes open, her eyes darting around and then landing on mine.

"Woah," she breathes out. "I think I passed out there for a second."

"Are you okay?" My brows furrow as I push the hair out of her face and look her over for damage.

"I'm so, so, good. I mean, I can't move, but I don't want to."

I take a deep breath, relieved she's not hurt, and then chuckle at her response. "I don't want you to move either," I murmur, circling my arms around her and sliding a leg in between hers. I want us tangled up forever.

After a few moments of peaceful silence, Ainsley turns around to face me, though I still keep her in my hold. Her teal eyes find mine, such love and contentment in their depths.

"I told you all about me, but what about you?" she asks softly, an adorable smile tugging at her lips.

"What would you like to know?"

"Everything," Ainsley sighs, curling up on my chest.

I chuckle and comb my fingers through her hair, letting the silky strands ground me in this moment. "You've seen my home, my land, and my animals. I'm really not much more complicated than that," I tell her, though deep down, I know there's more to my story.

I can't bring myself to tell her just yet. I need to make a phone call first and cash in a favor from an old friend. Once I know my Firefly is safe from her family for good, I'll tell her everything. I can't risk her freaking out and running right back to her awful family.

At least, that's how I'm justifying keeping a secret from Ainsley.

"What about your family? And friends? Tell me about your life," she encourages.

"It's just me up here these days," I start. "Used to live here with my ma and pa, but they passed on five years ago."

"I'm so sorry," she whispers, pressing a kiss to my chest. "I can tell you loved them very much."

I nod my head in confirmation. "Best people I ever knew." I swallow back the unexpected lump of emotion in my throat. "I wish they could have met you. They would've loved the stuffing right out of you, Firefly."

My girl giggles, her cute little nose scrunching up as laughter fills the room. "I want to hear all about them," she says, her eyes sparkling. "But first, can I ask what you do for a living? I mean, is that rude?"

"It's not rude," I tell her with a smile. "But even if it was, we don't care about social conventions up here, remember?" Ainsley smiles as she nods, then waits for my answer. "A lot of my time is spent keeping up the gardens and tending to the livestock. I also run a side business making furniture. Mostly rocking chairs and bed frames, though I also take custom orders."

"Really? Brewer, that's amazing! Can I see your work sometime?"

I grin down at my Firefly, loving the look of excitement and admiration in her teal eyes. It makes me damn proud of everything I've accomplished. I just hope she's still this enthusiastic when she finds out exactly how much money my "side business" makes.

Just then, Ainsley's stomach lets out an angry grumble. Her cheeks burn bright red, and I'm sure she's about to apologize. Instead, my girl pats her belly and looks toward the kitchen. "I'll wrassle us up some food," she says, hopping out of bed.

"Wrassle?" I ask, barely containing my grin.

Firefly shrugs, looking at me over her shoulder with the most adorable smirk. "Just testing out some new vocabulary words now that I'm basically a wild mountain woman."

This draws a chuckle out of me. "Test away, love. I'm going to make a quick call while you see what we have to eat?"

"You have a phone?!" she gasps.

"And internet," I confirm. "I need both for my business, though I won't lie, I forget to charge my phone more often than not."

"Could I make a call later? Not to my family. No way," she rushes to say. Ainsley makes a gagging motion and imitates throwing up. This woman. I know I'll never be bored around her.

"Of course. What's mine is yours, Firefly. You're not trapped here." She gives me a smile and a nod, pulling one of my shirts over her head as she waltzes toward the kitchen.

I dig around in the bedside table drawer for my phone, pleased when I find it with almost a full battery. Scrolling through the ten contacts I have, my thumb hovers over the name of the man I never thought I'd talk to again.

Valentino.

We met years ago when I lived in New York City. I happened to be walking across the street when he was jumped by four guys. I didn't think, I just dove in, ripping one man off of Valentino, then the next, until he was able to stand on his own. We took down his attackers together, and when all was said and done, Valentino said he had nothing to give me in thanks for saving his life. I didn't care. That's not why I did it.

Valentino told me he was working his way up in the family, and soon he'd have real power. It took me a second to realize what kind of *family* he was talking about. Still, Valentino was very serious about owing me a favor. Anything I wanted, as soon as he had the authority to make it happen. Over a decade later, and I never thought about cashing in. Until now.

I hit the call button, not sure what to expect. This phone number might not even be accurate anymore.

"Brewer? Is it really you?"

"Valentino," I say gruffly, more than a little shocked that he answered. "Wasn't sure you'd pick up. Hell, I wasn't even sure this was still your number."

"It's been, what? Ten years? Twelve?"

"Therin about," I answer. This is awkward, and I hate these kinds of interactions. Nevertheless, my Firefly needs protection, and this is the only way I know how to keep her safe. "I hate to cut straight to the chase, but this is a time-sensitive matter."

"No problem," he replies. "Is everything okay?"

"Is it too late to cash in that favor? You might not remember, but–"

"Of course, I remember. You saved my stupid ass on my first assignment." We both grunt at the memory of that day. "What do you need?" he asks after a moment of silence.

"There's a woman," I start. "More like an angel. A scared angel who has some secrets she thinks I can't handle."

"I can relate," he surprises me by saying.

"I need to know how to protect her. Can you look up information on people? I'm not sure what the scope of your influence is."

"Limitless."

I chuckle. "Good. I'm going to need you to do some digging on her family and their business interests. And, uh, maybe you could gather some... other intel?"

"Something that could be used to blackmail someone, perhaps?"

"Exactly."

"Text me all the info you have and I'll run it through our networks. Might take a day or two."

"Thank you, Valentino. I mean it."

"I owe you more than looking up information. You saved my life."

"This is all I need. Keeping my angel safe is the most important thing to me."

"Well then how about I settle for an invite to the wedding?"

"Deal," I grunt, making him suppress a laugh.

We hang up, and I wipe a hand down my face. I hope Ainsley understands. I need to make sure her family doesn't come after her, ever. She's mine now, and I'll always keep her safe.

Chapter 10

Ainsley

"Oh my god, Ainsley, is it really you?" my bestie says over the phone.

"Yes, yes, and I'm fine, I promise. More than fine, actually. I'm... stupendous. Deliriously happy. I didn't know life could be this... good," I say, finishing with a dreamy sigh. I know I sound like a silly school girl with a crush, but what Brewer and I have is so much more than that.

"Are you drunk?" Shay asks bluntly.

"No," I say with a laugh.

"High?"

"No, of course not!" I giggle. "I'm in looooove!" I sing-song. "And I'm free, Shay. Free from my parents, free from the complications of money and ridiculous expectations, free from everything."

"That sounds amazing, but I'm going to need some answers from you," she says matter-of-factly. "First, you didn't call, text, or FaceTime me for three days. Then, I finally work up the courage to call your mother, and she tells me you're a runaway bride! What the heck, Ains?"

"Wow, was that really only three days ago?" It's hard to believe I've fallen so deeply and irrevocably in love with Brewer in such a short time. I'm not scared, though. I feel like I've always loved him.

"Only?!" Shay exclaims. "Only three days of me going out of my mind! Only three days of me trying to get a hold of you every free moment I have, and getting scolded for having my nose buried in my phone!"

"I'm sorry, Shay," I tell her truthfully. I never meant to make her worry, and worse, I never want to be a reason her parents yell at her. I know all too well the kind of damage those words have, even though Shay would never admit it. "It all happened so fast. The wedding was sprung on me by my parents. I was standing there, looking down the aisle at the middle-aged man my dad hand-picked for me to marry, and something just... snapped."

"What do you mean?" Shay whispers. "God, Ains, I'm so sorry."

"I couldn't go through with it. Setting me up on disastrous dates is one thing, but an arranged marriage? I can't explain it, but I felt like... I felt like I crawled out of my skin and hovered over my body, watching the scene play out while not having any control over the outcome. Then, all at once, I took off."

"Took off?"

"I threw my bouquet on the ground, kicked off my heels, and ran right up the nearest mountain."

"You ran up a mountain bare-foot?"

"Yup. And I was almost attacked by a mountain lion, but my beastly mountain man came to my rescue."

"Ainsley! Tell me everything!"

I laugh, then dive into everything I've experienced the last few days. Well, almost everything. I keep the steamy details to myself.

There's shuffling in the background over the phone, then I hear Shay's mother screech, "Where are you? We need to get you ready for the cocktail party tonight."

My bestie groans, and my heart goes out to her. I know exactly what she's going through.

"Duty calls," she says sarcastically.

"You can run away, too," I whisper.

"And live with you and your mountain man in freaking Montana?"

"Hey, don't knock it," I say teasingly.

"I love you, Ains, but I'm a city girl through and through. Now if only I could convince my parents I can be a city girl all on my own without a man by my side."

"Maybe they're worried about you being alone after...?" I don't want to upset my best friend, so I don't reference her attack directly. She gets the hint.

"Worried?" Shay scoffs. "They have a hard time believing it even happened most days."

"I'm sorry, Shay. You need to get out of there. Or at the very least, start going outside of your comfort zone a little bit. You can build up the courage to leave one day at a time."

"Shay! I know you're in your room. Come out here this instant!" her mother snaps.

My friend groans, then tells her mom she's coming. "Gotta go," she sighs. "Thanks for calling and letting me know you're okay. We need to talk again ASAP, missy! I want a FaceTime call with you and your new beau."

I grin and agree to another call soon, though my heart aches for the life my bestie is trapped in.

After hanging up, I stand from the couch and stretch, lifting my arms over my head as I yawn.

"Trying to tempt me, Firefly?" Brewer asks, his voice low and filled with lust.

I turn and look over my shoulder, seeing my man lounging in a kitchen chair as his eyes roam over my body.

"Is it working?" I breathe out, rolling my body and shaking my hips. I'd feel silly, except the way Brewer is looking at me tells me everything I need to know. He loves the show, and wants more. I do, too.

My mountain man stands to his full height and prowls toward me, the fierce look in his hazel eyes causing my thighs to squeeze together. He closes the distance between us, tangling his fingers in my hair and pulling me head back so he can crash his lips down on mine.

"Always," he grunts before taking my lips again.

Brewer takes control of this kiss, walking us backward until my back is pressed up against the wall. He slides his tongue against mine, his hands roaming over my curves and clawing at my clothes. Brewer pulls me away from the wall and somehow shuffles us towards the bed while stripping both of us down.

Brewer takes a step closer to me, erasing the distance between us. He runs his hands up and down my naked body, caressing my hips, my breasts, even my throat and lips. His strong, capable hands leave a throbbing, warm blaze in their wake.

His hand wraps around the back of my neck, pulling me into him for a punishing kiss. I'm his. He owns every part of me. That's what he's telling me with each stroke of his tongue, each anguished groan that travels through his body and into mine. I feel his kiss everywhere, and I need more.

"Please," I whimper, not even caring that I sound desperate. I am. He's right there with me.

"I've got you, love. I've got you," he murmurs, gripping my hips and guiding me backward until the edge of the mattress hits the back of my legs. Brewer gently lays me out on the bed, then stands in front of me, looking down at my body. It's all for him.

I spread my legs, moaning when he growls and clenches his fist.

"Please," I whisper again, my hands trailing up my torso to cup my breasts. My skin is so sensitive, every light touch seems to go straight to my clit, making it throb in anticipation.

Brewer tears his eyes away from where they were locked on my pussy, and he grunts again when he sees me playing with my nipples.

"Fuck, Ainsley. You're so damn sexy." He's on me in the next instant, covering my body with open-mouthed kisses, sucking on my skin and leaving little love bites up my torso and on my breasts.

I jerk and twist beneath him, gasping for air and whimpering with each lingering touch and kiss. When he finally reaches my mouth, Brewer slants his lips over mine and leads us in a slow, drugging kiss.

My legs automatically spread wider so he can settle between them. I feel his long, thick cock glide against my pussy, collecting my juices and driving me crazy. He's so close to where I need him I nearly cry in frustration.

Brewer sits back slightly and gathers my wrists up in one of his massive hands. He raises my hands over my hand and pins them to the mattress before nuzzling into the side of my neck.

"Fuckin' love seeing you stretched out for me," he says into my skin, his voice low, gravelly, and desperate. Brewer drags his lips down my neck and across my collarbone, then he nips at the tops of my breasts, grinning wickedly when I jump and gasp. "Gonna fuck this sweet little pussy now, Ainsley. Are you ready for me?"

I nod and tilt my hips, nudging the swollen head of his cock against my entrance. Brewer growls and reaches down between us to guide himself inside in one smooth stroke. Fire spreads through my veins, and heat pulses out from my core, overwhelming my body.

I wiggle my hips, making sparks sizzle and burn across my skin. Brewer groans, leaning over me, one hand still holding my wrists above my head while the other trails up my side. He squeezes my breast, pinching my hardened, sensitive nipple before sucking it into his mouth.

My back bows off the bed, and he takes the opportunity to slip his hand between my back and the mattress, pushing my chest up so he can feast on me. Brewer grinds his cock into me, filling me up before pulling back and slamming into me roughly.

My breasts jiggle with every thrust as he sets a relentless pace. I wrap my legs around him and dig my heels into his sculpted ass, crying out when he hits that spot inside me that pushes me right up to the edge.

I feel my muscles tense as my pussy tightens around his thickness. He lifts his head from my chest and studies my face, no doubt sensing how close I am. My thighs shake and a shiver runs up my spine, seizing my lungs and forcing out a scream as I come around his cock.

Rivulets of pleasure course through my body, making every nerve ending spark to life. Brewer fucks me through it, never letting up. He still has my wrists secured in his grasp, despite all my writhing around and trying to twist away from the intense pressure and sharp ecstasy he's creating deep inside of me.

I swear I'm about to come again, but suddenly Brewer isn't on top of me anymore. I hardly have time to register his absence before his large hands grasp my hips firmly. Brewer flips me over effortlessly, then pulls my hips back so I'm on all fours.

"Fuck yes," he grunts, gripping my ass cheeks and spreading them wide.

Brewer thrusts into me, growling when he bottoms out. I let out a broken cry as I unravel for him, my orgasm ricocheting through my body but never leaving me completely. I'm so fucking sensitive, so raw as he pounds into me.

"I-I-I ca-ca-n't..." I stutter out, unable to take a full breath.

"You can, baby. Trust me, you can. Feel this with me. Fuck, feel it, Ainsley."

I whimper and nod my head, staying right here with him in the moment, struggling to hold myself up on shaky arms while my pussy knots around him over and over. Incoherent words and strangled, almost tormented sounds fall from my lips as Brewer tears me apart, fucks me so good, so hard, so damn rough. He's branding me with each savage stroke, claiming all of me, body and soul.

Brewer slides his hand around to my front, spreading his fingers out over my stomach and pulling me even closer to him as he ruts into me. His hand creates even more pressure.

My fingers curl into the sheets, fisting them as I try desperately to hold myself up. When he brushes the tips of his fingers over my clit, my knees wobble and my arms give out completely. I face plant into the pillow, my ass still in the air, Brewer still pounding away. He pinches my clit and I sob out yet another orgasm. My pleasure spikes as white hot bliss fills my veins. When it fades away, I'm completely limp. Boneless. Held up only by Brewer's punishing grip on my hips.

"Gonna come inside you, love. Gonna make you a mother," he growls as he holds himself deep inside me. His words make my pussy contract one last time, and that's his breaking point.

Brewer lets out a feral roar as his cum fills me up. He pulls back and then enters me again as more of his release shoots out of him. There's so much, I feel it dripping down my thighs, the tickling sensation making me moan and involuntarily tremble in his arms.

I feel the last of his orgasm drain from him, and then Brewer collapses on top of me. He's sweaty and panting for air as he rests his forehead between my shoulderblades. I feel his hot breath on my skin, the weight of his body on top of mine, his sweat mixing with mine, and I know.

I just... know.

Everything will work out as long as we're together.

Chapter 11

I feel the moment Ainsley relaxes and gives herself over to me and our future together. Pressing a kiss to her sweaty forehead, I roll to the side, dragging her with me. My firefly curls up on my chest and cuddles closer, while I wrap an arm around her and hold her against me.

The moment feels right to finally tell my woman how wealthy I am. Surely by now, Ainsley knows who I am, and knows I'd never be the shallow, selfish pricks her parents were, no matter how much I have in the bank.

I open my mouth to confess, when a loud banging on the door startles us both.

Ainsley gasps and reaches for the sheet to cover herself. I reluctantly slide out from underneath her, kissing her on the forehead. "Don't worry, love. I'll be right back. You stay here," I tell her before throwing on jeans and a t-shirt.

I grip the doorknob and take a deep breath. I'm pretty sure I know who's out there, and I don't want Ainsley to be any part of it.

Sure enough, I open the door to a pot-bellied man with an arrogant, indignant look on his red face. Ainsley's father, I presume.

"Who the fuck are you and where the hell is my daughter?!"

"I'm Brewer, and Ainsley is home now," I say calmly, stepping into the doorway so he can't get through. I cross my arms over my chest and stand to my full height, towering over the ruddy, portly man.

"The fuck she is. She's been missing for days, and I have it on good word she ran up this mountain. You're the first place I came to, and I have a feeling you know what happened to her."

"I do. She found her home right here with me, and that's where she's staying."

"So you admit you have her, *Brewer*?" he spits out, taking a step forward.

He looks like he's about to charge me, but then thinks better of it. I kind of wish he would. I'd love to knock this fucker on his ass, but I won't instigate violence against Ainsley's family. Unless she asks me to. In which case, I'd be more than happy to oblige.

"Yes. And I'm keeping her. She'll be my wife soon."

"She's already taken," the man snarls. "Or did she forget to mention that part before spreading her legs for a degenerate like you?"

I growl and clench my fists at my sides, taking two steps forward and crowding his space. "What the *fuck* did you just say?" My voice is low, but there's a threat laced in my words, one I know he picks up on.

"She ran away from her wedding," he says, puffing out his chest. He's trying to look intimidating, but the waver in his voice gives away his nerves.

"Then it sounds like she's not taken. Sounds like she didn't want to be married in the first place. In fact, from what she told me, it sounds like you used your own goddamn daughter as a pawn to make more money. That means you lost the right to be in her life unless she says so. It also means you lost the absolute privilege of taking care of her and supporting her and loving her the way she deserves to be loved."

"I-I, that's, well, that's just..."

"Enough," I growl, taking another step forward. The man takes a step back, nearly stumbling. "Get the fuck out of here. Don't come back or I'll have you arrested for trespassing."

This makes him laugh. A cruel, cold sound that I instantly want to choke out of him. "You think the cops are going to side with someone like *you* over someone like *me*? Face it, you're not good enough for her. You can't give her the lifestyle she's used to. She'll tire of her little backwoods adventure soon enough."

He sneers, probably expecting me to either be hurt at his comment or get angry. Instead, I laugh at him. "I love your daughter with everything that I am, and I know she loves me, too. That's all that matters. But if she wants me to lay the world at her feet, I can do that too. I make plenty of money with my handmade furniture business."

"Not enough," the man says, narrowing his eyes as a smirk stretches across his face.

"Actually, my net worth is ten percent higher than yours, Bartholomew Mcentire."

His face goes white at the same time a soft gasp sounds from behind me. *Shit.* Ainsley heard that. I know I should have told her sooner, but I couldn't think of a way to casually say that I'm a millionaire several times over. I don't *have* to live the simple life that I do, but I want to.

I can't worry about that right now though. First, I need to get rid of this asshole.

"And," I continue, "All of my income is legitimate. It's real money in the bank, not just empty promises to clients who trusted me with their life savings."

"What the... what exactly are you implying?" His voice is lower now, but his anger has tripled.

I grab the collar of his shirt and pull the pathetic man toward me, dragging him up to meet my gaze.

"You're not the only one with friends in high places," I grind out, staring into his soulless eyes. "And word on the street is that your investment firm is nothing but a ponzi scheme, old man."

"That's just, I mean, that's.... Preposterous. Slander, is what that is, Brewer."

"It's only slander if it's untrue. My source has plenty of records and bank statements to back up their claim. I'm sure your clients would be interested in seeing this information. Or perhaps the FBI?"

I watch as his face turns from furious to flustered, a deep satisfaction rolling through me. Valentino definitely came through with the information I needed.

Setting the man back down on the ground, he stumbles back a few steps before regaining his composure.

"Well now, just hold on a minute. I think we can come to some sort of agreement, don't you?"

Is he for fucking real right now?

"The only agreement I'll be making with you is that if you leave here right now and never come back or tell a soul what you found, then I won't completely destroy you. Don't get me wrong; I will be ending your career and blackballing you from every potential investor. You'll be stripped of your wealth and arrogance by this time tomorrow. *But*, if you leave here right now, I'll leave enough for you and your wife to settle into a nice apartment and find a job far away from the business world. Maybe a waiter or a custodian. Both admirable professions, and certainly more honest than your current career."

He gapes at me, wide-eyed and trembling. I see droplets of sweat forming on his forehead as he processes everything I've said. The man closes his mouth, takes a breath, and then opens it again like he's going to say something. I sear him with a deadly look, and the cowers before scrambling off in his fancy-ass car.

I watch him peel out, his car sliding on the gravel as he high tails it down the mountain. Once the dust trail disappears, I take a calming breath and prepare to face my angel. I pray she can forgive me for keeping my wealth a secret.

No sooner do I turn around than she's launching herself into my arms. I catch her easily and crush her into my chest as she wraps her arms and legs around me. "Did you mean it?" she whispers into the side of my neck.

"Yes. I've been successful in my business venture, and I hardly ever spend any money since the mountain provides everything for me. Add on to that some good investments that paid off in spades, and I'm a very wealthy man," I answer softly.

I brace myself for her disappointment or for her face to crumble with a look of betrayal. Instead, Ainsley shakes her head.

"Not that," she says dismissively. "The other part. About me being your wife soon?"

My heart just about bursts in my chest at her words. Of course my firefly doesn't care about my money. She cares about being mine, being home, being with me forever. I should have never doubted her.

"I've never meant anything more. As soon as you let me, I want to make it official. I know it's fast, but—"

"But it's true. It's real," she repeats the words I told her last night.

"So fucking real," I agree, kissing her all over her face.

Ainsley cups my cheeks and brushes her mouth against mine. I sip at her lips, then slide my tongue inside, savoring everything about her. She sighs so sweetly when we break apart, nuzzling into my neck and kissing me there. I love when she does that. I feel her smiling into my skin like she knows exactly what she's doing to me.

"We don't know everything about each other yet, but I know we belong together. I know you're not like my parents. You're nothing like the world I came from, and I love that about you. You're perfect for me."

Well, damn. My eyes sting with unshed tears. "I'm not perfect, Firefly, but I will love you better than anyone else."

"You already do," she whispers. "Thank you for rescuing me."

I cup the back of her neck and guide her face up towards mine so I can rest my forehead on hers.

"You, my beautiful angel, are the one who rescued me. You've given me everything, filled in my missing pieces, hell, you made more room in my heart just so you could fill that, too. I never want to be without you, not ever."

"I'm good with that," she says with a grin.

I can't help it. I kiss her soft, pouty lips again, pouring out my gratitude, love, and loyalty. I taste the same things on her tongue, both of us promising forever, right here on our mountain.

Epilogue

Ainsley

"And what's this one?" I ask my seven year old daughter, Eloise.

She scrunches up her cute little nose while studying the herb I'm pointing to. "Basil?"

"Yes!" I exclaim, clapping my hands.

We've been teaching our daughters about different plants and herbs that grow in the front garden. Eloise loves it, but our five year old, Maggie, couldn't care less. She's happily playing with her favorite dinosaur figurine in the dirt, so I don't bother her.

A cool breeze tangles in my hair, and I lift my head, enjoying the relief from the warm summer sun. It's hard to believe it's been eight years since I left my life behind and started on my adventure with Brewer. Each one has been filled with more love and laughter than the last.

We had a beautiful spring wedding as soon as the snow melted and the ground thawed. Shay came and was my maid of honor, and Brewer's mysterious friend from New York City made an appearance as well.

It was a small, intimate, and perfect ceremony. No frills, just the natural beauty of the mountain. My bouquet was composed of wildflowers which coordinated with my handmade daisy chain tiara. I walked down the aisle barefoot, which made Brewer nervous at first. I promised him it wasn't for an easy get away, it was just more comfortable and true to my new self. He was on board after that.

"What's next?" Eloise asks, her chipper voice breaking into my reverie.

"Hmm," I respond, tapping my chin with my finger. "How about this one?"

My daughter furrows her brow, concentrating on the shape of the leaves on the sprouts. "Par... par-less-y?"

"Parsley," I correct, smiling down at her. "It's a tricky word. I'll count it," I tell her with a wink.

Eloise beams up at me, then bends down and sniffs the parsley, sneezing when she inhales part of a leaf.

"Bless you," Brewer says, coming up behind me and wrapping his arms around my waist.

"Hi," I say to him, leaning against his chest. "I thought you'd be in your workshop all day."

"I really should be in there now, but I saw you and the girls out here, and needed to be here with you." My husband kisses my temple, then dips his head down to nuzzle into the side of my neck.

"We're always happy to have you," I whisper back.

"Daddy! I know my plants now!" Eloise practically shouts as she runs toward her father. He takes a step away from me, bending down and scooping up his little girl.

"Is that right?"

"Yup," she confirms, nodding her head.

"I'm so proud of you," he praises. Eloise giggles and wraps her arms around his neck.

Maggie, not wanting to be left out, stands from her dirt pile and barrels toward me. I don't hesitate to lean down and pick her up, dirty hands, muddy clothes, and all.

"I am here!" Maggie shouts once she's in my arms.

"Yes, you are," Brewer says with a chuckle, leaning forward to kiss her forehead.

"I'm pooped," she says with a sigh as she rests her head on my shoulder.

I laugh at her word choice. "Pooped?"

"Yeah. Daddy says it."

"Guilty as charged," my husband concedes.

Both girls snuggle up, Eloise in her father's arms while I cradle Maggie in mine. Looking over at Brewer, I see the love and gratitude in his eyes when they meet mine.

"I love you," I murmur.

"I love you so much, Firefly," Brewer whispers into the shell of my ear..

I still love his name for me, even after all these years. It's such a sweet reminder of how instantly my mountain man became obsessed in the best way possible. He always tells me the mountain brought me to him. All I know is that his love saved me, healed me, and made me whole.

Connect with me!

Check out my website, cameronhart.net[1], for sneak previews on my latest projects.

Follow me on social media:

Facebook Page - facebook.com/cameronhartauthor
  Instagram - instagram.com/cameron.hart.author
  TikTok - tiktok.com/@author.cameron.hart
  Goodreads - goodreads.com/16081533.Cameron_Hart
  Bookbub - bookbub.com/authors/cameron-hart

---

1. https://cameronhart.net/

Also by Cameron Hart

Check out my other popular series and books!
Mafia, MC, & Bodyguard Romance:
Moscatelli Crime Family Series[2]
Di Salvo Crime Family Series[3]
Chaos MC series[4]
Savage Ride[5]
Mountain Man Romance:
Men of Blackthorne Mountain Series[6]
Bear's Tooth Mountain Men Series[7]
Cowboy & Small Town Romance:
Roped in by Love Series[8]

2. https://books2read.com/u/mqBaze

3. https://books2read.com/u/m0odzW

4. https://books2read.com/u/bMVAOk

5. https://books2read.com/u/bMVlG7

6. https://books2read.com/u/3RYDvB

7. https://books2read.com/u/mVel7A

8. https://books2read.com/u/3RYlBY